INTERFACT ™

THE BOOK AND DISK THAT WORK TOGETHER

PLANTS

TWO CAN ™

CHANHASSEN, MINNESOTA · LONDON

Book and disk by
act-two Ltd

Published by Two-Can Publishing,
18705 Lake Drive East, Chanhassen, MN 55317
1-800-328-3895
www.two-canpublishing.com

ISBN: 1-58728-460-X

2 4 6 8 10 9 7 5 3

'Two-Can' and 'Interfact' are trademarks of Two-Can Publishing.
Two-Can Publishing is a division of Creative Publishing international, Inc.
18705 Lake Drive East, Chanhassen, MN 55317

Photographic Credits: Front cover: Planet Earth Pictures
Biofotos: p9 tr, p13 tr, p24 tl, p25 tr; Bruce Coleman: p8, p10, p13 bl, p15, p19;
Michael & Patricia Fogden: p28; Hutchison: p31 tl;
Science Photo Library: p16 bl, p19 br, p23 b, p26 cl, p27 br;
ZEFA: p 6, p9 l, p11, p16 r, p19, p23 t, p24
Illustrations by Nancy Anderson

Printed in Hong Kong by Wing King Tong

INTERFACT

THE BOOK AND DISK ▽ THAT WORK TOGETHER

INTERFACT will have you hooked in minutes –
and that's a fact!

● The disk is packed with interactive
activities, puzzles, quizzes and games
that are great fun
to do and full of
interesting facts.

Find the hidden
pairs and match
each plant to the
thing it grows from.

Click on
the pots
and find
the pairs

● Open the
book and discover
more fascinating
information
highlighted with
lots of full-colour
illustrations and
photographs.

Do you know
how plants make
their own food?
Read up and
find out!

● To get the most out of **INTERFACT**,
use the book and disk together.
Look out for the special signs,
called Disk Links and Bookmarks.
To find out more, turn to page 43.

23

BOOKMARK

DISK LINK
Put your
**GREEN
FINGERS** to
work and grow
your own plant on screen!

Once you've clicked on to
INTERFACT, you'll never
look back.

LOAD UP!
Go to **page 40** to find out how to load
your disk and click into action.

What's on the disk

HELP SCREEN

Learn how to use the disk in no time at all.

These are the controls the Help Screen will tell you how to use:

- arrow keys
- text boxes
- "hot" words

GREEN THUMB

Plant a pea and watch it grow on your screen.

Grow your own virtual pea plant on screen. Watch a tiny seed turn into a flower, and learn each stage of a plant's development. But take good care of your little plant – or it will die!

THE GLOSSARY GAME

Check out this snappy word game!

A friendly fly is winging its way toward the jaws of a Venus's flytrap. See if you can figure out a mystery word before the hungry plant gets its lunch.

THE GREEN GLOBE

Take a look at different plants around the world!

Basil the Botanist is your guide as you go globetrotting in search of interesting plants from around the world. Find out what grows where!

KNOW-IT-ALL GNOMES

Get the answers to all your questions about plants.

Why are plants so important to the environment? What conditions do plants need to grow? These gnomes know it all. All you have to do is ask!

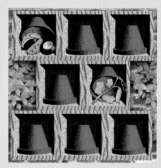

POT LUCK

Drive yourself crack-pot crazy with this wild match-up game!

See if you can match each plant to the thing it grew from before your time runs out. Once you've found all the pairs, learn more about seeds, bulbs, and tubers.

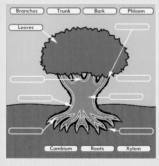

TREE-MENDOUS

Investigate a tree – from top to bottom, inside and out!

Start by dragging all the name tags into the right positions. Then click on each one and learn more about the different parts of a tree.

BUZZ OFF!

Are you a botanical whiz kid? Check out this super plant quiz!

Put your plant expertise to work and help the busy bee pollinate a flower. If you finish the quiz in time, you'll find out all about pollination.

What's in the book

Looking at plants

Scientists believe there are over 260,000 **species** of plants around the world. Plants grow in all sorts of environments – from cracks in the sidewalk to deep in the ocean. Some types of plants are able to grow in the hottest, driest deserts. Others survive in the coldest, iciest regions of the world. Plants are adapted to suit the conditions in which they live.

▲ The largest flower in the world is a type of rafflesia. It is 3 feet (1 m) across and smells of rotting meat! It grows in the rain forests of Indonesia. Rain forests are home to more plant species than any other **habitat**.

◀ Trees are the largest living things on the earth. Some trees grow slowly and can live for a very long time. Bristlecone pines, which grow in the south-western United States, are among the oldest living things in the world. Some of these trees are 5,000 years old!

▲ Some plants have adapted to life in rivers, ponds, and seas. A few water plants are so small that they can be seen only with a microscope. Some types of water plants and seaweed have pods of air in their branches that lift them up to the light near the surface of the water.

DISK LINK
There's a whole world of plants to explore in **THE GREEN GLOBE.**

◄ About half of all the world's plant species are flowering plants. They come in all sorts of shapes, colors, and sizes. Many flowers are brightly colored, and some of them produce powerful scents.

Liquid magic

Plants must have exactly the right conditions in order to grow. The first ingredient for survival is water. All plants need water – without it they will shrivel up and die. Some plants live in or under water. Others, such as cacti, survive in hot, dry deserts by storing water for long periods.

▶ Make a pond in an old bowl, or dig a hole and line it with a piece of tough plastic. Add stones or shape the sides so that they are shallower than the middle. Fill your pond with water. After a few days, put in some pondweed and other water plants. Keep an eye on your pond to see what other types of plants start to grow.

▲ Many desert plants have fleshy stems and leaves that store water. This is a huge welwitschia plant, which is found in the Namib Desert in Africa.

DISK LINK
Make sure your virtual plant gets the right amount of water in GREEN THUMB.

▼ Plants in pots can die if you water them too much. Desert cacti prefer dry soil, so water them only occasionally. Other plants prefer damp soil.

▲ Water lilies can grow in deep ponds because they have long stems. The **roots** are at the bottom of the pond, and the leaves float on the surface.

Light fantastic

Plants use light to make the food they need in order to grow. Different plants need different amounts of light. Some plants grow in hot countries, where there are few clouds and the sun shines brightly. Others grow in shady places, such as woods, and need less light to survive. But no plant could survive without any light at all!

▼ Slide a sleeve of cardboard over the leaf of a potted plant. Leave the plant near a window for a week, then take off the paper. What has happened to the leaf?

▶ Most plants have green leaves. This is because they contain a **pigment** called **chlorophyll**. Chlorophyll enables the leaves to absorb light and make food. But not all leaves are plain green! Some have other colors in them, such as white or red. Leaves such as these are called variegated leaves.

▼ The plants in these window boxes get plenty of sunlight to help them to grow.

▲ Seedlings are small, young plants. They need plenty of light to develop and grow. Different amounts of light change the way plants grow. Place a pot of seedlings on a windowsill and stand a piece of cardboard behind it. What happens to the seedlings? What happens if you turn the pot around?

Breathing in and out

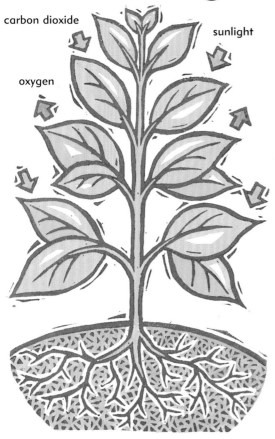

carbon dioxide

sunlight

oxygen

Plants use carbon dioxide to make food. But they need oxygen, too. Plants use oxygen to break down their food and turn it into energy.

▼ Put some pondweed in a jar. Put the jar upside down in a bowl of water. Leave it in a sunny spot for several hours, and you will see bubbles of oxygen collecting in the jar.

Plants need food in order to grow – just like you do! Plants make the food they need in a process called **photosynthesis**. Inside a plant's leaves, a substance called chlorophyll takes in energy from sunlight. This energy is then used to turn water and carbon dioxide into sugar. A waste product of this reaction is oxygen, which the plant releases into the air. So plants take in carbon dioxide, the gas your body produces when you breathe out, and they release oxygen – the gas you need in order to breathe!

◀ Put a clear plastic bag over a plant, then seal it around the stem with string. A few hours later the sides of the bag will be covered in small droplets of water. This water has escaped through tiny holes in the plant's leaves. These holes are for absorbing carbon dioxide, and water loss is a side-effect.

DISK LINK Remember what you learn on these pages to help you save the fly in **THE GLOSSARY GAME.**

▶ Mangrove trees grow in swampy, coastal areas. At low tide, their **aerial roots** are exposed above the salty sea. These trees absorb some of the gases they need through their roots.

◀ In addition to air, light, and water, plants need **minerals** to grow. Some plants can't get the minerals they need from the soil. So they catch insects and digest the minerals from their bodies. Here, a fly lands on a Venus's flytrap. It brushes against sensitive hairs and triggers the jaws of the plant, which close and trap it.

15

Flower power

Flowers come in all sizes, shapes, and colors. Many flowers have markings to guide visiting insects into the proper position to pick up or deposit **pollen**.

▲ Bees are attracted to the nectar inside flowers. They use nectar as food and, as they digest it, they make honey.

DISK LINK
Do you have flower power? Then help the bee in BUZZ OFF!

▲ Many plants and animals live together in harmony. This hummingbird is drinking **nectar** from a flower. As it drinks, pollen sticks to its body. The hummingbird helps to spread the pollen by carrying it from flower to flower.

▼ Flowers are attractive to people, too. Many flowers, such as jasmine, have scents that are used to make perfume. Try experimenting with the fragrances of different flowers. Ask permission to gather sweet-smelling leaves and flowers from garden plants, such as rosemary, lavender, or roses. Dry the petals and leaves between sheets of blotting paper, then arrange them in a bowl.

petal

stamen

sepal

▲ Pollen is made up of tiny grains that contain male cells. These join with female cells inside a flower and form **seeds**, which grow into new plants. Pollen is carried between plants by the wind, insects, birds, and bats. This process is called **pollination**.

You should not pick wildflowers. Many of them are rare and are protected by law.

Waiting to grow

Some seeds have parachutes or propellers to help them fly on the breeze. Other seeds hook onto fur, or are eaten by animals and end up in their droppings.

▲ Plants such as mosses, **fungi,** and ferns grow from **spores** instead of seeds. Take a look at the underside of a fern leaf. The brown lumps you see produce a dust that is made up of millions of spores. These spores are sometimes carried by the wind over great distances.

◄ Each seed is surrounded by a protective coat. In some plants, such as cherries, this outer layer is very hard. Cherry seeds are also covered by soft **fruit**, which is often eaten by birds. The seeds pass through the birds' bodies and fall to the ground in their droppings. Plants such as tomatoes and apples have many seeds inside each fruit. If conditions are right when the seed reaches the ground, it splits open and starts to grow. Many seeds have a built-in food supply that the plant uses until it grows and is able to make its own food.

DISK LINK
Use these pages to help
you match the seeds to
the plants in POT LUCK.

▼ Chestnuts are seeds. Squirrels often bury chestnuts in the ground to use as a winter food supply. Sometimes, the squirrels leave some of their supply behind. In spring, the forgotten chestnuts start to grow.

▲ Pine cones have seeds stored inside them. In dry weather, the cones open to release their seeds.

▼ Mushrooms are a type of fungus. They grow from spores. To see these spores, remove the stalk of a mushroom and leave it, gills down, on a piece of paper overnight. The spores in the gills will leave a pattern.

Always ask an adult if mushrooms or other fungi are safe before you handle or eat them.

Bean feast

Some seeds grow inside pods. When the seeds are ripe, the pods burst open and send the seeds shooting off. Depending on where they land, it may take months, or even years, until the conditions are right for the seeds to **germinate**. Seeds need water, warmth, and oxygen to start growing. Some seeds also need light.

DISK LINK
Read these pages carefully. Some of the words will help you save the fly in THE GLOSSARY GAME.

▼ Make a sprouting potato head! Take a large potato and hollow a hole out of one end, then fill it with mustard and alfalfa seeds. Cut up vegetables to make ears, eyes, and a nose and attach them with toothpicks. The water in the potato will make the seeds sprout. After a few days, you will have a funny, hairy face.

▼ Wet a sheet of clean paper towel, roll it loosely, and put it in a jar. Then place a fresh broad bean between the glass and the paper, roughly in the middle of the jar. In a few days, the seed coat should begin to split. Each day, mark the side of the jar with a felt-tip pen to show how far the shoot and root have grown. Roots travel downward searching for water. Shoots grow in the opposite direction, looking for light. The root and shoot know which way to grow by sensing **gravity**.

▲ Soak a cupful of mung beans in water. Drain them and put them in a jar. Twice a day, pour a little water in the jar, shake it gently, then tip the water out. The seedlings use food stored in the bean to grow leaves and roots. In five days, the shoots should be ready to eat in a salad.

▶ Try growing apple, orange, lemon or melon seeds. Soak the seeds overnight in a saucer of water left in a warm place. The next day, plant them in twos or threes in yogurt containers filled with potting compost. Water them well and put the pots in a warm, shady place until shoots appear. Be patient – fruit seeds take a long time to germinate. Keep the soil moist, but do not make it too wet or the seeds will rot. Re-pot the seedlings as the plants get larger.

Roots and runners

Tubers, rhizomes, and **bulbs** are underground food stores that help some plants survive the winter. A potato tuber swells in summer to store food for the plant to live on in winter. The following spring, the potato tuber sprouts into life.

New plants can be grown from the leaves or stems of a parent plant. Strawberry plants send out long stems called runners, which start to grow roots. In this way, new plants can grow a good distance away from their parent plant.

◀ Place a hyacinth bulb in the neck of a jar filled with water so that the bottom of the bulb is wet. Leave the jar in a dark place until the shoot is about 1 inch (3 cm) high, then bring it into the light. A fragrant flower will grow from the bulb.

DISK LINK
See if you can find the tubers and bulbs on
THE GREEN GLOBE.

▼ Wild bluebells also grow from bulbs.

◀ Tulips grow from bulbs. Bulbs store food for the plant in winter, and the flowers bloom in spring.

▼ Garlic is an edible bulb.

Magic minerals

Most plants have roots that absorb minerals and water from the soil. The water travels to all parts of the plant through tubes, just like blood in veins.

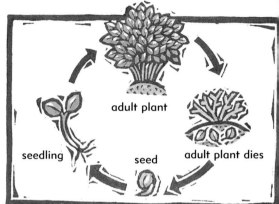

adult plant

seedling

seed

adult plant dies

▲ Roots not only absorb water and minerals, they also help to anchor plants firmly in the soil. The roots of this mountain **conifer** manage to grip the thin soil between the rocks of a cliff.

▲ Over a long period, a plant uses up lots of minerals from the soil. After the plant has died, it rots and breaks down, releasing minerals back into the soil. If a seed germinates near the same spot, its roots feed on the minerals left by the earlier plant.

◄ Dead leaves that fall to the ground also put minerals back into the soil. Over several years, the leaves decay and make a layer of compost, called leaf mold. Worms drag some leaf mold down into the soil, making it richer for plants.

DISK LINK
Get some expert advice
on soil from the
KNOW-IT-ALL GNOMES.

▶ You can make compost
to improve the soil in
your garden or window
box. Save soft vegetable
matter, such as old potato
peelings, and mix it with
grass and leaves in a plastic
box with a lid. In about five
weeks, this will rot into a rich,
brown mass. Mix it with soil to
feed to all your different plants.

Be very careful
not to cut yourself
when peeling
vegetables.

▲ Animals help to add
minerals to the soil
through their droppings.

25

Terrific trees

A tree is a tall plant with a woody stem that grows to a height of at least 16 feet (5 m) above the ground. It has a trunk and branches that are covered in **bark**, which protects the tree from pests and stops it from losing too much water.

▲ You can tell the age of a tree by counting the number of rings across its trunk. Every spring, a tree grows a thick ring of new wood under its bark. In summer, a thinner ring of darker wood grows. These two rings together show one year of the tree's growth. If the rings are wide, it shows that the tree was growing quickly. If the rings are narrow, it shows that the tree was growing slowly.

DISK LINK
Take a close-up look at the different parts of a tree in **TREE-MENDOUS.**

◀ **Evergreen** trees have green leaves all year long. The leaves of **deciduous** trees change color and drop off in the autumn. Collect a variety of leaves. Lay each leaf under a sheet of paper and rub gently with a wax crayon. Label your rubbings and put them in a scrapbook.

◀ Tack some paper to a tree trunk and rub over it with a wax crayon. Add the bark rubbings to your scrapbook.

▼ Trees have grown on the earth for millions of years. These insects were trapped in the sticky **resin** oozing from damaged bark about 30 million years ago. Fossilized resin is called amber.

Balancing act

Trees and plants help life on earth. They provide food for people and animals. They also recycle water and some of the gases in the air. When forests are cut down, the balance of nature is disturbed.

DISK LINK
The **KNOW-IT-ALL GNOMES** have more to tell you about the earth's environment.

▲ Carbon dioxide is poured into the earth's air by factories, homes, and cars. Plants reverse this process by absorbing carbon dioxide and releasing oxygen. But as the earth's forests are cut down, more carbon dioxide will build up in the air. One of the results of this could be global warming!

◀ Rain forest plants soak up water with their roots and release it into the air through tiny holes in their leaves. This keeps the air moist all year long.

▶ Make a rain forest bottle garden and watch the process in action in your own home!

To make your own mini rain forest, you will need the following:

● A large, wide-necked jar.

● A tight-fitting lid or cork.

● Some tiny pebbles or gravel, rinsed and cleaned.

● Damp compost.

● A spoon or fork with a stick tied to the handle.

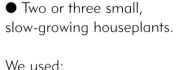

● Two or three small, slow-growing houseplants.

We used:

polka dot plant

bead plant

silver net plant

1. Clean and dry the jar. Cover the bottom with gravel for drainage.

2. Spoon a thick layer of compost over the gravel. Dig holes in the compost and put the plants in place with the spoon. Tap down the soil around the roots and water the plants.

3. Seal the jar and put it in a place where it will get lots of light. Water the bottle garden only once a month. The mist that forms on the glass is water being given off by the plants.

Glorious food

Plants are an important source of food for people all around the world. We get energy from vegetables, fruits, and seeds. Some people, called vegans, eat only plant matter. But even meat-eaters feed on animals that eat plants!

▲ This shows how plants help to feed animals and people. Unlike other living things, plants make food for themselves. **Herbivores** and **omnivores** eat plants, while **carnivores** eat animals.

DISK LINK
Discover the food crops of the world when you explore **THE GREEN GLOBE.**

◄ Seeds provide energy for people and animals. You can make a winter treat for the birds. Just mix some birdseed in a bowl with some fat. Put it in an old dish and leave it on a windowsill or bird feeder.

▼ Tea is made from the dried leaves of tea bushes, which are grown on large plantations. It is one of the most popular drinks in the world.

▲ This woman is planting rice seedlings. Rice is the main food for half of the world's people. Other seeds that we eat include peanuts, peas, beans, wheat, oats, and corn.

◄ Many fruits and vegetables contain essential vitamins. Most of the vegetables that we eat are **annual** plants that live for just one season. **Biennial** plants sprout and grow one year, then produce fruit and die the next. Plants that live for many years are called **perennials**.

Colorful creations

In addition to food, plants provide wood, cork, paper, rubber, and materials to make rope, cloth, furniture, and matting.

▼ To make colorful eggs, ask an adult to boil some eggs for five minutes in water with onion skins, beets, or spinach added to it. For a patterned egg, paint on it when it has cooled and dried.

 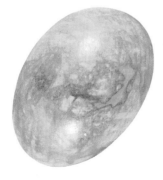

eggs dyed with onion skins

▲ Wool that has been tinted with natural dyes is being sold in this street stall in Bolivia. For centuries, plant juices have been used to make many colorful dyes. Today, most dyes are made artificially.

▶ Herbs and spices make food tasty. They come from the different parts of plants, such as seeds, roots, or leaves. Saffron strands are part of a crocus flower.

▼ You can make your own colored stationery and gift wrap by tinting sheets of pale, absorbent paper or thin cardboard. Ask an adult to boil a large quantity of onion skins or beetroot in a pan. Carefully strain the water into a clean basin. When the water is cool, dip in the sheets of paper. Peg the dyed paper to dry on a line. Experiment with other brightly colored plant matter, such as spinach or rhubarb. What color dyes do these plants make?

DISK LINK
Have you read these pages carefully? Then you're ready to BUZZ OFF!

Glossary

plants for a bottle garden

Aerial roots are roots that are exposed above the ground.

Annuals are plants that live for one year, or one season.

Bark is the protective outer casing on the woody parts of a tree.

Biennials are plants that live for two years.

Bulb is a resting bud surrounded by short, thick leaves. Food is stored in the bulb.

Carnivore is an animal that eats other animals. A tiger is a carnivore.

Chlorophyll is the green pigment that plants use to combine sunlight, water, and carbon dioxide to make food.

Conifers are evergreen trees that produce cones. The cones are filled with seeds.

Deciduous trees shed their leaves in the autumn.

Evergreen trees have green leaves throughout the year.

Fruit is the part of a plant that contains the seeds. Many fruits have juicy, sweet-tasting flesh. This helps to attract animals, which eat the fruit, then deposit the seeds in their droppings.

Fungi are neither plants nor animals, according to some scientists. The group includes mushrooms and toadstools. Unlike most plants, fungi do not make their own food. They live mainly on the rotten remains of other plants.

Germinate is to cause a seed to sprout. This occurs when the conditions for growth are exactly right.

Gravity is a force that pulls things toward the ground.

Habitat is the natural home of a living thing, or a group of living things. For example, a river or a forest is a habitat.

Herbivore is an animal that eats only plant matter. Cows are herbivores.

Minerals are solid, nonliving substances. Living things need minerals to help them survive and grow.

Nectar is a sugary liquid produced mainly by flowers. Insects, birds, and bats are attracted to nectar, and this helps to spread pollen from flower to flower.

Omnivore is an animal that eats both plant and animal matter. Most people are omnivores.

Perennial is a plant that lives for many years.

Pigment is a substance in plants that produces color.

Pollen is the yellow dust produced by a flower's stamen. It contains the male cells needed to fertilize the female cells in a flower to make seeds.

Pollination is the transfer of pollen from one flower to another.

Photosynthesis is the way in which plants create their own food. They combine chlorophyll and sunlight with water and carbon dioxide to make the energy they need to survive.

Resin is a sticky substance that oozes out to heal wounds in the bark of some trees.

Rhizome is a thick stem with scaly leaves that grows horizontally underground. Plants such as ferns, irises, and many grasses produce rhizomes.

Roots are the part of a plant that anchor it in the ground. They absorb water and minerals from the soil.

Seeds contain a new plant that develops during germination. They also contain a store of food for the new plant.

Species is a group of plants or animals that look similar and behave in similar ways.

Spores are tiny capsules that will grow into new plants. Ferns, mosses, and fungi develop from spores.

Tubers are short, swollen stems that develop underground. They contain a store of food. New plants can grow from buds on a tuber. A potato is a tuber.

Lab pages

Photocopy these sheets and use them to make your own notes.

Lab pages

Photocopy these sheets and use them to make your own notes.

Loading your INTERFACT disk

INTERFACT is available on floppy disk and CD-ROM for both PCs with Windows and Apple Macintoshes. Make sure you follow the correct instructions for the disk you have chosen and your type of computer. Before you begin, check the system requirements (inside front cover).

CD-ROM INSTRUCTIONS

If you have a copy of INTERFACT on CD, you can run the program from the disk – you don't need to install it on your hard drive.

PC WITH WINDOWS 95

❶ Put the disk in the CD drive
❷ Open MY COMPUTER
❸ Double click on the CD drive icon
❹ Double click on the icon called PLANTS

PC WITH WINDOWS 3.1 OR 3.11

❶ Put the disk in the CD drive
❷ Select RUN from the FILE menu in the PROGRAM MANAGER
❸ Type **D:\PLANTS** (Where D is the letter of your CD drive)
❹ Press the RETURN key

MACINTOSH

❶ Put the disk in the CD drive
❷ Double click on the INTERFACT icon
❸ Double click on the icon called PLANTS

FLOPPY DISK INSTRUCTIONS

If you have a copy of INTERFACT on floppy disk, you must install the program on your computer's hard drive before you can run it.

PC WITH WINDOWS 95

To install INTERFACT:
1. Put the disk in the floppy drive
2. Select RUN from the START menu
3. Type **A:\INSTALL** (Where A is the letter of your floppy drive)
4. Click OK – unless you want to change the name of the INTERFACT directory

To run INTERFACT:
Once the program has been installed, open the START menu and select PROGRAMS, then select INTERFACT and click on the icon called PLANTS

PC WITH WINDOWS 3.1 OR 3.11

To install INTERFACT:
1. Put the disk in the floppy drive
2. Select RUN from the FILE menu in the PROGRAM MANAGER
3. Type **A:\INSTALL** (Where A is the letter of your floppy drive)
4. Click OK – unless you want to change the name of the INTERFACT directory

To run INTERFACT:
Once the program has been installed, open the INTERFACT group in the PROGRAM MANAGER and double click the icon called PLANTS

MACINTOSH

To install INTERFACT:
1. Put the disk in the floppy drive
2. Double click on the icon called INTERFACT INSTALLER
3. Click CONTINUE
4. Click INSTALL – unless you want to change the name of the INTERFACT folder

To run INTERFACT:
Once the program has been installed, open the INTERFACT folder and double click the icon called PLANTS

How to use INTERFACT

INTERFACT is easy to use.
First find out how to load the program
(see page 40), then read these simple
instructions and dive in!

You will find that there are lots of different features to explore.
To select one, operate the controls on the right-hand side of the screen. You will see that the main area of the screen changes as you click on different features.

For example, this is what your screen will look like when you play Know-It-All Gnomes, in which the garden gnomes will answer all your questions. Once you've selected a feature, click on the main screen to start.

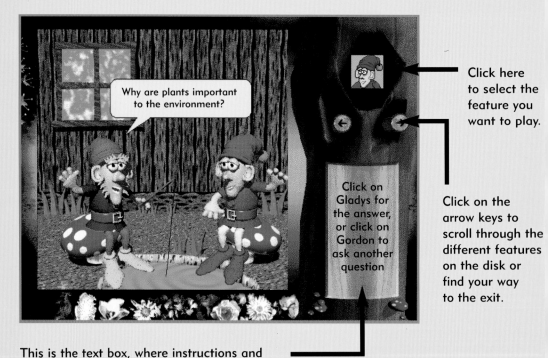

Why are plants important to the environment?

Click on Gladys for the answer, or click on Gordon to ask another question

Click here to select the feature you want to play.

Click on the arrow keys to scroll through the different features on the disk or find your way to the exit.

This is the text box, where instructions and directions appear. See page 4 to find out what's on the disk.

DISK LINKS

When you read the book, you'll come across Disk Links. These show you where to find activities on the disk that relate to the page you are reading. Use the arrow keys to find the icon on screen that matches the one in the Disk Link.

DISK LINK
Find the biggest, smallest, oldest, and tallest plants on
THE GREEN GLOBE!

BOOKMARKS

As you explore the features on the disk, you'll bump into Bookmarks. These show you where to look in the book for more information about the topic on screen. Just turn to the page of the book shown in the Bookmark.

23

LAB PAGES

On pages 36–39, you'll find pages to photocopy. These are for making notes and recording any thoughts or ideas you may have as you read the book.

HOT DISK TIPS

- After you have chosen the feature you want to play, remember to move the cursor from the icon to the main screen before clicking the mouse again.

- If you don't know how to use one of the on-screen controls, simply touch it with your cursor. An explanation will pop up in the text box!

- Keep a close eye on the cursor. When it changes from an arrow ➔ to a hand, ☞ click your mouse and something will happen.

- Any words that appear on screen in blue and underlined are "hot." This means you can touch them with the cursor for more information.

- Explore the screen! There are secret hot spots and hidden surprises to find.

Troubleshooting

If you have a problem with your INTERFACT disk, you should find the solution here. You can also e-mail for help at info@creativepub.com

QUICK FIXES Run through these general checkpoints before consulting COMMON PROBLEMS (see opposite page).

QUICK FIXES PC WITH WINDOWS 3.1 OR 3.11

1 Check that you have the minimum system requirements: 386/33Mhz, VGA color monitor, 4Mb of RAM.

2 Make sure you have typed in the correct instructions: a colon (:) not a semi-colon (;) and a back slash (\) not a forward slash (/). Also, do not put any spaces between letters or punctuation.

3 It is important that you do not have any other programs running. Before you start **INTERFACT**, hold down the Control key and press Escape. If you find that other programs are open, click on them with the mouse, then click the End Task key.

QUICK FIXES PC WITH WINDOWS 95

1 Make sure you have typed in the correct instructions: a colon (:) not a semi-colon (;) and a back slash(\) not a forward slash (/). Also, do not put any spaces between letters or punctuation.

2 It is important that you do not have any other programs running. Before you start **INTERFACT**, look at the task bar. If you find that other programs are open, click with the right mouse button and select Close from the pop-up menu.

MACINTOSH

1 Make sure that you have the minimum system requirements: 68020 processor, 640x480 color display, system 7.0 (or a later version), and 4Mb of RAM.

2 It is important that you do not have any other programs running. Before you start **INTERFACT**, click on the application menu in the top right-hand corner. Select each of the open applications and select Quit from the File menu.

COMMON PROBLEMS

Symptom: Cannot load disk.
Problem: There is not enough space available on your hard disk.
Solution: Make more space available by deleting old applications and files you don't use until 6Mb of free space is available.

Symptom: Disk will not run.
Problem: There is not enough memory available.
Solution: *Either* quit other open applications (see Quick Fixes) *or* increase your machine's RAM by adjusting the Virtual Memory.

Symptom: Graphics do not load or are of poor quality.
Problem: *Either* there is not enough memory available *or* you have the wrong display setting.
Solution: *Either* quit other applications (see Quick Fixes) *or* make sure that your monitor control is set to 640x480x256 or VGA.

Symptom: There is no sound (PCs only).
Problem: Your sound card is not Soundblaster compatible.
Solution: Try to configure your sound settings to make them Soundblaster compatible (refer to your sound card manual for more details).

Symptom: Your machine freezes.
Problem: There is not enough memory available.
Solution: *Either* quit other applications (see Quick Fixes) *or* increase your machine's RAM by adjusting the Virtual Memory.

Symptom: Text does not fit neatly into boxes and "hot" copy does not bring up extra information.
Problem: Standard fonts on your computer have been moved or deleted.
Solution: Reinstall standard fonts. The PC version requires Arial; the Macintosh version requires Helvetica. See your computer manual for further information.

Index